The Whispering Lake

A Haven Hollow Mystery

by Lula Starling

Published by The Gilded Garden
Winter Haven, Florida

ISBN: 979-8-9943557-5-6
Cover design: Lula Starling
Printed in the United States of America

Dedication

For those who listen when the water speaks—
who know that silence has a language of its own
and that memory moves like current beneath calm surfaces.

And for those who have stood at the edge of something vast and still,
hearing their own name carried back on the wind.

May you find peace in the places that once held your restlessness,
and learn to trust the whispers that lead you home.

They say the lake remembers everything—

but I've come to believe it chooses what to keep.
Some memories it hides beneath the reeds,
others it carries on the wind until someone listens.

No one warns you that water can watch.
It studies faces leaning over it,
takes impressions like glass cooling in a mold.
It holds on to the words we think are gone,
and one day, when the air is thick and the light feels strange,
it gives them back.

The people in Haven Hollow say the lake is peaceful now.
They say the bridge washed away the stories with it.
But sometimes, just before dawn,
I hear the water breathe.
It isn't loud—just a sigh that ripples through the cattails,
like the sound a secret makes when it's ready to be told.

This is the summer the lake decided to remember me.

THE HAVEN HOLLOW CHRONICLE

Est. 1914 — Serving the Chain Since the Boom
August 12, 2025

RIBBON-CUTTING MARKS NEW ERA FOR HAVEN PIER

By Marianne Ellis, Staff Writer

Haven Hollow — A crowd gathered Thursday evening to celebrate the ribbon cutting of The Haven Pier, a waterfront redevelopment project billed as "a return to the Hollow's golden age." The Northern Line Investment Group — a team of out-of-state developers from up north — calls the Pier a revitalization of Haven Hollow's heritage.

Locals, however, remember that heritage differently. The new Pier stands on the rubble of the town's original ferry dock, once the beating heart of lake life during the 1920s boom. In its day, the old dock was more than a launch — it was an event. Travelers waited for ferries beside neon-lit diners and open-air pavilions. Families made a night of it, watching the lake shimmer under carnival lights while jazz from the Gilded Hotel drifted across the water.

Those who recall that era say the new development feels more imitation than homage.

"They think they're reinventing something that never really died," said Earl Maddox, 82, a lifelong resident and one of the last whose father worked the ferry line. "The lake just got tired of carrying all that noise for a while."

Construction was delayed several times due to what contractors called "unexpected flooding." Equipment left overnight on-site was found adrift by morning — or missing entirely. The developers blame "soil saturation." Locals have another theory.

"The water remembers where it ran before," said Maddox, half-smiling. "Sometimes it just comes back to check."

Despite the talk, the Pier opened to fanfare and flash photography. But some of the older residents who gathered for the ribbon cutting noted that the new lights glared off the lake in a way that felt—unsettling.

For the record, Chronicle archives confirm that the same shoreline once held The Link Bridge, a narrow wooden crossing that connected the ferry landing to the opposite bank. It was lost during the Great Storm of 1926, just weeks before the fire that destroyed the original Gilded Hotel downtown.

Whether coincidence or history repeating, the lake now reflects another promise of progress—one built, once again, upon its past.

Chapter One

The House by the Links

The first morning in the new house smelled faintly of paint and rain. Outside, the Links murmured their steady language against the reeds—not loud, just present, like a conversation that had started long before she arrived.

Ivy stood barefoot on the porch, coffee cooling between her palms, watching the mist slide across the water. The surface looked almost solid from here, a sheet of glass stretching toward the faint lights of the Haven Pier across the lake. In daylight it would be picturesque, the kind of view that sells a dream. At dawn, it looked older—something breathing beneath its own reflection.

She'd fallen in love with the view the moment she saw it in the listing. The agent had called it lakefront serenity, and after years of highway noise and windowless offices, that had sounded like salvation. More than that, it had sounded permanent.

Growing up, home had never stayed the same for long. After her mother remarried, every house seemed to come with a new promise and a new reason it wouldn't last. Rent went up. A job disappeared. Another move. Another set of boxes stacked in a hallway while somebody swore this place would be different. Ivy had spent too much of her life learning not to get attached to walls.

This house was different because it was hers. No landlord. No packed-up kitchen in the middle of the night. No waiting to see what somebody else might ruin. If she kept it standing, it would stay.

She tightened both hands around her mug, then frowned and glanced back through the open door toward the kitchen. Had she locked it after letting Shadow in? She was already halfway through the thought before she caught herself. Typical. Her mind always ran ahead of her body. Grocery lists, invoices, things she needed to do tomorrow before she had even finished today.

She wasn't what people called a water person—she didn't swim, didn't boat, didn't crave the open expanse. Not after the near-drowning when she was twelve, all chlorine and panic and somebody else's weight dragging her under while no one noticed fast enough. Even now, water unsettled her in ways she couldn't explain. She loved looking at it. Loved the quiet of it, the way it made the world feel larger and slower. But there were days when even a narrow bridge over a shallow creek could make something cold slip down her spine, as if she might look over the edge and see something looking back.

The lake lay smooth beneath the morning mist. Peaceful. Beautiful.

And for one brief second, before the breeze disturbed the surface, Ivy had the strange feeling that something beneath it had been watching her watch it. What she wanted was the stillness—the light breeze that kept the air moving, the hush that felt like permission to rest.

This morning, though, the stillness felt different. Not peaceful. Held.

As the mist thinned, Ivy noticed something strange about the yard. The grass at the lake's edge didn't taper naturally toward the water. It rippled once, then stopped.

The sod along the shoreline had settled in uneven squares, faint seams still visible beneath the grass. One section near the edge bulged slightly higher than the rest, the ground beneath it warped in a shallow wave, as though something older had been covered over instead of removed.

Beyond it, the earth ended too abruptly. Not softened by reeds or cattails, not sloping gradually into the lake. It simply stopped, as if someone had drawn a line and told the land to end there.

The drop was barely three feet, but the water below it looked too deep, swallowing the shoreline without any margin between earth and dark.

She crouched near the edge. The exposed roots along the bank spread through the soil in thick, tangled webs, some disappearing beneath the water, others twisting downward into the dark where the lake had pulled back. They did not stop where the shoreline stopped. They reached farther, as if the trees remembered when the water had once been somewhere else.

Looking at it made something tighten low in her chest. The whole yard had the feeling of a room after the furniture had been moved—familiar in shape, wrong in every detail.

She stepped back and took another sip of coffee, telling herself she'd ask about it later. Maybe the developer had filled part of the land. Maybe the lake had taken some back. Around here, people said most lakes were old sinkholes anyway—bottomless in their own way.

The wind shifted, carrying the scent of lavender from the garden mixed with something faintly metallic. Across the water, the Haven Pier's lights flickered in the fog, their reflections breaking into restless threads. For a moment, the ripples almost looked like they were reaching toward her porch.

Ivy turned away first.

She slipped on her shoes and decided to walk the property line, circling the house like she might circle an idea she wasn't ready to name. Dew clung to the edges of the grass, silvering her footprints as she moved. The lavender bushes lining the porch bent with the breeze, releasing their perfume in soft, uneven breaths. The smell was clean but heavy, the kind that settles into the fabric of a place—the kind that lingers after visitors leave.

As she rounded the back of the house, the light shifted from gold to gray. The canal that fed the Links ran parallel to the fence line, its water slow and dark, carrying leaves like tiny boats. On the other side of the canal, she could just make out the outline of Marla's cattle field—a pale blur of fences, feed sheds, and the lazy shapes of animals grazing in the distance. Their low moans rolled across the morning air, steady as church bells, anchoring the scene in something alive and ordinary.

It was peaceful in a way that unnerved her.

Every few steps, Ivy paused, scanning the yard for anything out of place—cracks, sinkage, debris. The only sound was the shifting of the breeze and the faint creak of the wind chime she hadn't hung. She didn't own a wind chime.

The noise came again, faint but clear, somewhere near the back corner of the property—a metallic note brushing through the lavender.

Ivy followed it, eyes on the ground this time. Halfway there, the edge of her flip-flop caught on something hidden beneath the dirt.

She stopped short and jerked her foot back.

A rusted iron hook curved up from the ground beside the lavender bed, half-buried and easy to miss. Another step and she would have come down on it hard. For a second she could almost feel it punching through the thin sole of her sandal and into her heel.

"God," she muttered, pulse jumping. "That would've been a tetanus shot."

She crouched. The hook looked old enough to belong to another house entirely. Most of it disappeared beneath the dirt, buried deeper than it should have been, as though someone had simply built around it instead of taking it out. A short rusted chain still hung from the curve, shifting faintly in the breeze.

She brushed dirt from the metal. The iron was strangely cold beneath her fingers.

A small tag still clung to the chain by a corroded loop. As the light shifted off the lake, it flashed suddenly—not bright, but sharp, the kind of glint that made her flinch before she knew why.

Ivy leaned closer. Something had once been stamped into the tag. Most of it had worn smooth with age, but there was still the faint outline of a mark beneath the rust. Not quite a number. Not quite a letter. It looked oddly familiar anyway—the kind of symbol she imagined might have marked an old dock post or ferry line decades ago.

Behind her, Shadow let out a low sound.

Ivy looked toward the porch. He stood frozen near the screen door, ears flat, tail puffed, staring not at her but at the hook.

When she reached toward it again, he hissed. Whatever words had once been there were gone.

For a moment, she thought about pulling it free and taking it inside. But with Shadow still staring at it from the porch, the idea of disturbing it made her hesitate.

Instead, she let the dirt fall back over part of the buried hook and stood. The short length of chain shifted once in the breeze, the rusted tag turning just enough to catch the light again before going still.

As she walked back toward the porch, the breeze picked up again, carrying the lavender's sweetness over the darker scent of the lake—mineral, deep, and ancient.

She paused at the edge of the yard one last time.

The surface of the canal had gone completely still. No breeze touched it. No bird skimmed across it.

Then, near the center, a single ripple spread outward.

Ivy frowned. Nothing had disturbed the water.

In the center of the widening ring, the reflection changed.

For a heartbeat, the canal no longer reflected the neighboring docks and fences across the water. Instead she saw dark pilings, a narrow wooden pier stretching farther into the lake than any modern dock, and beyond it the outline of a long, low building with a peaked roof and lantern light burning in the windows.

The Haven Pier. But not as it was now. Older.

Then she blinked.

The image folded inward, as though something beneath the water had pulled it down.

The ripple vanished.

The canal reflected only sky again.

It wasn't a shoreline, she realized. It was a line someone had drawn—a line in the sand. And she couldn't tell which side she stood on: the one meant to stay put, or the one daring to cross.

Chapter Two

Low Tide

The days began to find their rhythm.

By the third morning, the house no longer smelled like cardboard and fresh paint. It smelled like her—coffee, lavender, and the faint trace of lemon cleaner that drifted in every time she opened the porch door. The echo inside the rooms was softening, replaced by the creak of wood under her steps and the quiet hum of ceiling fans.

Ivy liked that sound. She liked most of the sounds here. The buzz of cicadas. The distant low of cattle from across the canal. The occasional hum of a boat motor far out on the Links. They gave the air a kind of ordinary life that city noise never did—less demanding, more conversational.

Outside, the lake shimmered in its usual silence. Mornings here had a rhythm too: fog lifting, birds trading places, wind teasing ripples across the surface like a hand smoothing wrinkles from silk. It was all deceptively peaceful—the kind of peace you don't question when you've been chasing it for years.

By midmorning, Ivy had slipped into her new routine—open the blinds, brew her coffee, water the porch plants, then unpack a few more boxes. She'd painted the guest room the day before, a pale sage that changed color with the light. Today, she planned to tackle the study—the room facing the lake.

She was dragging another box toward the hallway when a deep plastic rattle caught her ear. It rolled past the front window, low and hollow—the sound of a bin bumping down asphalt. She froze for a second, realizing what day it was.

"Trash day," she murmured, half to herself.

She set the box aside and hurried outside, slipping into her sandals. The air was bright and already warming, cicadas starting their midday chorus. Down the street, a green bin clattered to a stop at the curb, and the woman pushing it waved like she'd been waiting for this very moment.

"You must be the new neighbor," the woman called out, smiling. "You're just in time. They'll skip you if you miss it."

"Thanks," Ivy said, pulling her own bins from the side of the house. "I didn't even realize it was Thursday."

"Easy mistake. Happens to everyone their first week."

Ivy hauled her bins to the curb, stacking the flattened moving boxes into the blue recycling cart. "Which one's which again?" she asked, already guessing wrong.

"Blue for recycling, green for garbage," the woman said. "Think of it as sky and earth. If you put trash in the sky bin, they'll leave it behind. Learned that one the hard way."

Ivy laughed, brushing a strand of hair from her face. "Noted. I'll try to keep the elements in order."

The woman grinned, and when she laughed, it came out unexpectedly soft and bright—more like a little girl's giggle than the laugh Ivy had expected from someone sunburned and practical in muddy garden shoes.

"I'm Marla," she said. "Been here long enough to know all the quirks. Four houses down, blue shutters, mailbox that's leaning because my late husband swore every year he was going to fix it and then never did." She smiled at the thought, but there was something wistful beneath it. "Now I leave it crooked out of spite."

She lowered her voice a little, like she was about to share a secret. "My only real complaint is the ducks. Everybody thinks they're charming until they start stealing pet food off your porch and glaring at you like you owe them money."

Ivy laughed.

"And don't let anybody tell you the lake's quiet when the weather changes," Marla added. "Folks around here say if you hear bells out on the water and there isn't a boat in sight, you stay inside."

She giggled again and waved one hand. "That's just old Haven Hollow nonsense, though. Every town has to have something to blame besides humidity."

"I'll keep that in mind," Ivy said.

"What about you?" Marla asked. "What brought you all the way out here?"

Ivy hesitated, then shrugged. "Honestly? I wanted someplace quieter. I write for a living, and I thought maybe if I could hear myself think for once, I might actually finish something."

"Well," Marla said, smiling, "you definitely picked the right town for thinking. Maybe not always for sleeping."

"Just moved in Saturday."

“Well, welcome to Haven Hollow,” Marla said, resting her hands on the bin handle. “We’re quiet around here—nosy but friendly. I’m four houses down, the one with the cat who thinks he runs the block.”

They talked for a few minutes—about the pickup schedule, the noise from the Pier, and how the lake always smelled different after a storm. Marla pointed out the best hardware store, the day the mail came early, and which neighbors kept snacks out for the ducks.

As they chatted, Ivy found herself relaxing in a way she hadn’t expected. Marla’s voice carried the rhythm of the town itself—unhurried, gently amused, like she had nowhere better to be.

When they finally said goodbye, Ivy lingered at the curb, watching the street shimmer under the heat.

Marla started back toward her house, green bin rattling behind her. Halfway up her driveway, she stopped.

Instead of going inside, she turned toward the narrow strip of grass behind her house where the canal met the lake. She stood there for a moment, looking out across the water as if she'd heard someone call her name.

Then, faintly, from somewhere behind Ivy's house, came the hollow metallic note of the buried hook brushing against its chain.

Marla looked up sharply toward the sound.

Just for a second, the easy expression slipped from her face.

Then she smiled again, waved once more, and disappeared inside.

Across the lake, the lights of the Haven Pier began to blink on one by one.

Ivy wrapped her arms around herself, unsure if the chill that moved through her came from the wind or the water.

Chapter Three

The Drop-Off

That night, rain arrived without warning.

Not a storm—just a steady, unhurried whisper that began somewhere over the lake and spread across the roof until the whole house sounded like it was breathing. Ivy drifted in and out of sleep, lulled by the rhythm, half-dreaming she could hear the water speaking in syllables she almost recognized.

By morning, the rain had passed. The air outside glowed silver, the world rinsed clean. The smell was sharp—ozone and damp lavender bending under its own weight. Drops clung to the screens like glass beads, and the lake had crept closer, the waterline brushing the base of her yard's slope.

She carried her coffee to the porch, letting the screen door sigh shut behind her. The boards were cool beneath her bare feet. Across the water, the Haven Pier shimmered faintly through a sheet of mist, its new lights blurred to pale halos.

When she reached the edge of the yard, she noticed the line again. It looked different this morning—sharper, more defined. The grass had receded another inch, not washed away but sliced, like a clean break. The soil beneath was dark and compact, threaded with something pale and angular.

She crouched and brushed the top layer of mud aside with her fingertips.

Beneath it, the soil changed. The ground under the grass felt packed too firmly, flatter than it should have, like something solid lay just below the surface. When she pressed harder, her fingers struck wood.

Ivy froze.

Not a root. Not a rock.

She cleared away a little more mud. For an instant she could see the edge of a weathered board beneath the dirt, dark with age and laid perfectly straight. Another ran beside it, separated by a narrow gap.

They looked less like debris and more like the remains of something built.

A walkway.

Or the slats of an old dock.

Her breath caught. The boards seemed to run beneath the grass toward the canal, as though the shoreline had once stretched farther out and someone had buried whatever had stood here.

Then the lake shifted.

Water lapped suddenly at the drop-off, and when she looked back, the boards were gone beneath the dark mud again.

She stood, coffee forgotten, scanning the shoreline. The faint curve of the pattern followed the property's border, perfectly straight until it met the canal fence. She tried to remember if the inspection mentioned any sort of retaining wall, but nothing about this looked modern.

Not because she had seen those exact boards before, but because for one strange second, crouched there at the edge of the yard, she had the dizzy feeling that she was standing at the end of a dock.

The sensation came so suddenly that her stomach dropped. She could almost feel water on every side of her, dark beneath her feet, and herself one step away from falling in.

She drew back too fast, breath catching painfully in her throat. Chlorine. Panic. A boy's shoulder driving her under. The helpless, awful moment of opening her mouth and swallowing water instead of air.

Ivy pressed one hand hard against the damp grass until the feeling passed.

She shook her head. “Coincidence,” she said quietly.

The faint hum of a mower drifted across the street, followed by the steady bark of a dog and the rhythmic slap of a screen door. Morning life returning to Haven Hollow.

Ivy spent the next few hours painting the study. The pale sage looked softer now, the color of misted glass. She opened the windows to let the scent of paint escape, and a cool breeze rolled through, carrying the low murmur of water against stone.

She paused mid-stroke, brush hovering. The sound was steady, rhythmic—not the gentle lap of waves but a deeper, more deliberate pulse, like water striking something hollow.

She moved to the window.

Near the drop-off, the lake's surface had gone strangely smooth. No wind touched that patch of water. No ripples crossed it.

Then, slowly, something appeared beneath it.

At first she thought it was only shadow. But the longer she stared, the more distinct it became: narrow, parallel lines just below the surface, dark and straight and evenly spaced.

Boards.

Not floating. Fixed.

They stretched away from her yard beneath the water in a narrow path, disappearing into the fog.

For one impossible second, Ivy knew—with the same certainty you know you are falling in a dream—that if she stepped outside and followed them, they would lead her to the end of an old dock.

Her skin prickled. Goosebumps raced up both arms.

The room suddenly felt too warm, the air too thin. Her throat tightened with the memory of water where air should have been.

She blinked hard.

The lines vanished. Only fog remained.

Ivy exhaled slowly and set the brush down. "Old construction," she said to no one. "Foundation, maybe."

But the explanation rang hollow even as she said it.

By late afternoon, the sun broke through, warming the damp air. The lavender swayed in the breeze, releasing its sweetness across the porch. She poured another cup of coffee and sat outside, trying to lose herself in the quiet.

Across the lake, laughter drifted from the Haven Pier—the sharp, high sound of children, followed by the echo of music and clinking glasses. The sound carried easily across water, thin and clear.

She thought of what Marla had said: The lake gets glassy after sunset. Looks like it's breathing.

Now, in the shimmer of fading light, Ivy could almost see it—the faint rise and fall of the surface, the slow inhale and exhale of something vast and unseen.

Her gaze drifted back to the drop-off, to that precise, impossible line.

If this had once been part of the old pier, then the water that touched her porch tonight had touched those stones more than a century ago.

And if the stories were true—that water remembers—then maybe it remembered everything that happened there.

She didn’t realize she was shivering until her coffee trembled in the cup.

Some say the lavender grew where the boards once met the shore, marking the line between what was built and what was taken back.

Chapter Four

Lavender and Smoke

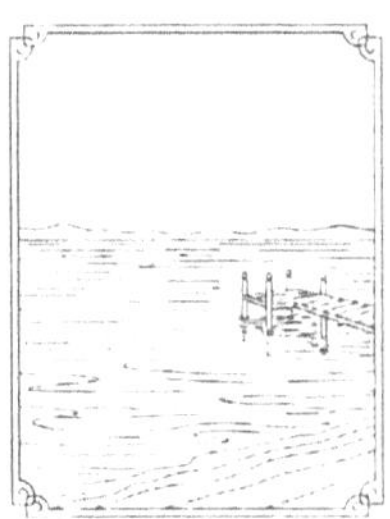

The morning sunlight spilled across the kitchen like a soft admission of peace. For once, the world outside didn't feel like it needed tending. Ivy stood at the counter, waiting for the coffee maker's final sigh, her fingers tapping absently against the Formica.

Shadow wound between her ankles, tail flicking, patient in that entitled feline way. "All right, I hear you," she said, filling his bowl before taking her own first sip. The coffee was still too hot, but she liked the sting—it made her feel awake, present.

The faint smell of new paint had nearly vanished now, replaced by the lake breeze drifting through the open windows. It carried a softer sweetness—the lavender that bordered the porch—boosted by sunlight and the slow warmth of the morning. The scent mingled with salt, humidity, and the faint metallic tang that always came from water meeting air.

It was supposed to be a calming scent. Today, it just reminded her of the edge of things—the blurred line between control and surrender.

She opened her laptop, intending to look for curtain rods. Instead, her cursor hovered over the bookmarked property records website.

She hadn't meant to check again. Everything had already cleared—the inspection, the flood zone, the insurance, all of it. She'd done her research months ago, poring over maps, calling county clerks, asking the kind of questions that made people say, *you're thorough.*

But the thought of that perfect, unnatural line at the back of her yard had been needling at her all morning.

She typed her parcel number into the search bar and hit enter. The first few pages came up as expected: deed transfers, developer filings, insurance bonds. Clean, organized. But when she clicked the tab for **Historical Surveys**, the page went blank.

"File not found," the screen said.

She refreshed. Tried again. Same result.
She entered her neighbor's address. *File not found.*

For a long moment, she didn't move.

Records didn't disappear.

They were misplaced. Archived. Corrupted. But not erased.

She had built her adult life on documentation — contracts, inspections, disclosures, verification. She had done everything right before buying this house. Called the county twice. Pulled flood maps. Asked about prior claims.

There had been proof.

There was always proof.

The idea that something this foundational could simply not exist unsettled her more than the shifting waterline ever had.

Something tightened behind her ribs.

Every time she thought she'd built something solid, life found a way to move the ground.

She picked up her phone and called the county office. A cheerful woman answered, and Ivy explained the missing files.

“Oh, that happens sometimes,” the woman said. “Some older plats were lost in a municipal fire in the 1930s. Happens with a lot of our records.”

Ivy frowned. “But Haven Hollow’s fire was in 1926.”

“Maybe a different one. I can put in a request, but it might take a few weeks to see if we can locate backups.”

Ivy thanked her and hung up.

Her throat felt dry. She realized she hadn’t spoken a single word since waking, but her mind had been talking nonstop—thoughts circling, dissecting, convincing, replaying. All that silent noise left her parched. She took a sip of her coffee; it had gone cold.

I did everything right, she thought, the words quick and clipped inside her skull, the way a heartbeat starts to trip when it forgets its rhythm.

I did everything right, she thought, the words quick and clipped inside her skull, the way a heartbeat starts to trip when it forgets its rhythm.

She had spent most of her life making sure she would never have to start over like that again. Working early. Saving when she didn't have much to save. Choosing carefully—jobs, apartments, relationships. Watching other people make reckless decisions and promising herself she wouldn't be one of them.

Stability had never been something she assumed. It was something she built.

Degree. Career. Clean record. No missed payments. No disasters she didn't see coming first.

She had followed the rules so closely she could recite them.

And still, somehow, the ground shifted.

And yet here she was again, with something slipping through her fingers.

The Haven Hollow Historical Society sat on the corner of Central and Vine, a squat brick building whose windows always looked half asleep. Inside, the air smelled like dust and ink—old paper exhaling.

A woman at the desk—silver hair, large glasses—looked up as Ivy entered. "Morning," she said. "You're new."

"I moved to the lake a few weeks ago," Ivy said. "I was hoping to find some old records about the property. I heard some were lost in a fire."

"Some?" The woman smiled faintly. "Try most. The Great Fire took the original archives and half the block besides. We've been rebuilding ever since."

"I was told my parcel's history was unavailable online."

"What address?"

Ivy gave it, and the woman's expression shifted slightly. "Oh," she said softly. "You're on that side of the lake."

The words landed differently than they should have.

Ivy felt it before she understood it—the faint shift in the room, like a draft passing through a closed space.

"What's that supposed to mean?"

Mrs. Leary didn't answer right away. She studied Ivy over the rim of her glasses, her gaze sharper now, less casual. Not unfriendly. Just… aware.

"Nothing bad," she said at last, though her tone had changed. "Just—most of those lots weren't part of the original plats. That land used to belong to the old ferry dock. Back then they called it The Landing."

She paused, then added more quietly, "Some places take longer to settle than others."

Ivy held her gaze. "Settle?"

Mrs. Leary's smile returned, but it didn't quite reach her eyes this time. "On paper, I mean. Records, boundaries, all of that."

Another pause. Then, almost as if she couldn't help herself:

"You'll notice things, living there."

The statement hung between them a second too long.

Mrs. Leary straightened, the moment passing. "You won't find much on paper. But I might have something. Come back tomorrow?"

Ivy nodded. "Thank you, Mrs. Leary."

The woman smiled, surprised. "You know my name?"

"It's on the plaque by the door."

"Sharp eyes. That'll serve you well around here."

The drive home cut through the oldest stretch of Haven Hollow. Live oaks arched over the road, their branches tangled with Spanish moss that swayed like breath. The air shimmered with late-afternoon heat.

As she turned toward the lake, the new Haven Pier came into view—its metal frame gleaming under the sun, glass storefronts catching the light. The sign across the front read: *Rebuilt on the Promise of Renewal.*

She slowed, watching people move along the boardwalk. Families, couples, children with ice cream cones. The laughter carried across the water—thin, cheerful, distant.

For a fleeting second, she imagined standing on her own side of the lake, decades ago, when the world was sepia-toned and alive with carnival lights. Ferries docking, jazz drifting over water. It must've felt endless then, before the smoke and sirens came.

By the time she reached home, the sky had shifted to gold.
The lavender along her walkway shimmered in the wind, its scent thick in the humidity. She brushed her hand over the blooms and felt the oil cling to her skin.

The porch was her favorite place—half shelter, half threshold. She lit a citronella candle and set it on the rail. The flame hissed, then steadied, releasing that clean, citrus tang that tangled with the floral air.

The smell of Florida evening—sharp, alive, not gentle but honest. A chorus of cicadas began somewhere in the trees.

She leaned back, letting the rhythm of the evening settle in her chest.

Across the lake, the Haven Pier lights blinked on one by one. Their reflections wavered like distant fires on the water's surface. For a moment, she imagined the lake breathing again—slowly, deeply, as though remembering how.

Maybe the records were gone because of the fire.
Maybe because some stories weren't meant to be retold.

Either way, it wasn't her fault. She had done everything right.

The citronella burned steady—then flickered.

The flame bent, not away from the lake as the breeze should have pushed it, but toward it.

Ivy stilled.

The lavender shifted in the opposite direction, brushing softly against the porch rail.

The air moved one way.

The flame moved another.

Out on the water, a single ripple crossed the lake without a sound.

For the first time that day, Ivy didn't reach for an answer.

She just let it be.

Chapter Five

Echoes in the Water

The mornings had begun to fall into rhythm. Coffee, porch, a slow check of the mail she didn't expect yet. Shadow had claimed the wide sill by the front window, his tail twitching in time with the chirps outside.

Ivy liked the predictability. It made her feel as though she'd finally reached the part of life that moved without hurry.

Today, though, the quiet felt heavier—like the air was waiting.

She stepped outside with her mug and turned toward the lake. The wind had gone still. The lavender by the steps hung motionless, and across the water the Haven Pier's flags drooped against their poles. The whole scene looked pressed flat under glass.

Then she heard it—soft and rhythmic, like distant hammering.

Three beats.

Silence.

Three beats again.

Ivy didn't move.

The sound was faint enough that she might have missed it if she'd been thinking about anything else. But now that she'd heard it, she couldn't unhear it.

Three slow, measured taps.

She set her mug down carefully on the porch rail and leaned forward, listening.

The lake remained perfectly still. No boats. No wind. No movement along the far shore.

Three beats again.

This time, closer. Or maybe just clearer.

Ivy held her breath, trying to place it. Construction? Pipes? Something knocking loose under one of the docks?

But the sound didn't echo the way it should have. It didn't carry across the water.

It felt... contained.

As if it wasn't coming from across the lake at all.

Three beats.

Then nothing.

When it stopped, the silence didn't return to normal. It pressed in tighter, like the sound had left something behind.

Later that morning, Ivy decided to walk the loop that circled the small canal behind the last row of houses. She'd started doing it most mornings—a way to stretch, clear her head, and quietly take inventory of the neighborhood she was still learning to call home.

The air smelled faintly of grass and sun-warmed water.

She followed the paved path toward the mailbox cluster at the end of the lane. A few houses down, she slowed. The canal had thinned again. What used to be a smooth, reflective surface now lay patchy with mud and mirrors of shallow water.

The birds were there—the same ones she'd seen before. Spoon-billed and still, lined up with military precision along the edge. They stood like they were waiting for orders, not food.

Ivy watched them for a moment, transfixed by their stillness. Then a movement farther down caught her eye.

A man sat on the bank behind one of the houses, a fishing pole angled loosely over the water.

Ivy slowed.

The canal was too shallow here—more mud than water, broken into thin reflective patches that barely moved. There was nothing in it worth catching.

And yet, there he was.

Barefoot. Still.

His legs were folded beneath him, posture too straight to be relaxed. The line from his rod dipped into water that couldn't have been more than a few inches deep. It didn't move.

Two dogs sat a few feet behind him.

They weren't playing. Weren't sniffing or pacing. They sat the same way the spoon-billed birds stood—alert, silent, waiting. Their eyes fixed on the water.

The birds lined the opposite edge of the canal in a perfect row. None of them moved.

It felt less like a scene and more like a command.

Ivy kept walking, slower now.

As she drew closer, the man turned his head.

His eyes caught the light—and for a split second, they reflected it the way an animal's would. Not bright. Not glowing. Just wrong enough that her brain hesitated trying to place it.

The dogs' eyes did the same.

Ivy's chest tightened.

She told herself it was just the angle of the sun.

The man watched her approach without speaking.

His face… shifted.

Not dramatically. Not enough to point to.

Just enough that every time she looked at him, something about it felt different.

The lines in his forehead seemed too deep for his age.

Then normal.

His nose—slightly too long.

Then not.

His mouth curved faintly, almost a smile, but it stretched just a little wider than it should have.

Then it was gone.

Ivy slowed to a stop a few feet away, unsure why she had.

“Morning,” she said, because that was what people said.

The man tilted his head, studying her.

“You must be new around here.”

His voice was even. Calm. Almost polite.

But it didn’t sound like a question.

It sounded like a conclusion.

Ivy nodded once. “Just moved in.”

He looked past her then, toward the lake behind her house.

For a moment, his expression settled into something that almost resembled recognition.

Then it was gone.

"It takes people a while," he said.

"To get used to it."

Ivy frowned. "Used to what?"

The man didn't answer.

He turned back to the water.

The line in his fishing rod remained perfectly still.

The dogs did not move.

The birds did not move.

Ivy stood there one second too long, waiting for something—movement, explanation, anything that would make the scene feel normal again.

Nothing came.

She nodded once more, though he wasn't looking at her anymore, and continued down the path.

She could feel his gaze on her back.

She didn't turn around.

Not until she reached the mailboxes.

And even then, when she finally looked—

He was still there.

Exactly as before.

Watching.

She realized then she'd been holding her breath.

Back home, Ivy placed her mail on the counter, unopened. The sound of her footsteps echoed slightly off the new floors. She glanced toward the porch, half expecting to see the man's reflection across the water.

Instead, the lake looked calm again—too calm.

She told herself it was nothing. People fished in shallow water all the time. Maybe he was just catching bait. Maybe the birds were drawn to the same thing he was.

But she couldn't shake the image: the birds standing still, the man unmoving, the faint ripple that had spread through the water when she'd passed.

That afternoon, while folding laundry, she caught herself humming—a nervous habit she hadn't done in years. It was the same three-beat rhythm she'd heard that morning.

She stopped, heart quickening, and listened.

Outside, the wind had picked up again. The lavender swayed, the chimes clinked softly, and across the water came that same faint knocking sound—three slow, measured taps, like someone working deep beneath the surface.

Shadow lifted his head, ears turning toward the sound.

Ivy whispered, half to herself, "Please tell me that's a boat."

But no boat moved on the lake.

Chapter Six

The Water Remembers

Ivy woke before dawn to the sound of dripping.

It wasn't raining—she could tell by the rhythm. Rain was erratic, alive; this was measured and patient, like the tap of a metronome. For a moment she thought it was in her dream, until Shadow lifted his head from the foot of the bed and flicked an ear toward the window.

She swung her legs out of bed and padded to the hallway. The air was cool and thick, carrying that faint metallic scent again—the same one she'd noticed when the tide first began to lower.

The dripping led her to the porch. Dew slicked the boards, and the citronella candle from last night sat cold and spent on the railing. Beyond it, the lake lay utterly still. The waterline had shifted again, just barely, like the surface had exhaled overnight.

The hammering she'd heard yesterday echoed faintly in her mind.

Three beats. Silence. Three beats again.

She pressed her palms to the porch rail and whispered, "What are you trying to tell me?"

Later that morning, she drove to the Historical Society. Mrs. Leary was waiting near the counter, a manila folder in her hands.

"I told you I'd find something," she said. "Though this might not be the kind of something you want."

Ivy managed a smile. "I'll take anything at this point."

Mrs. Leary slid a thin clipping across the desk. The paper was yellowed, the ink faint but legible. At the top, in serif letters, it read:

Accident at The Landing – Ferry Fire Claims Four Lives

Ivy's heart stumbled as she read. The article was brief—just a few paragraphs describing a ferry blaze that broke out near the dock's end sometime around 1893. The cause remained unknown. The names of the dead were listed, though only one stood out: Edwin Vale, a craftsman noted for "his fine stonework and an unfortunate habit of working by lantern light."

"That was before Haven Hollow was even a town," Mrs. Leary said softly. "Back when this was just The Settlement."

"Do we know what caused the fire?"

"Records say it started from oil lamps." Mrs. Leary's fingers tightened slightly on the edge of the folder. "But my grandmother used to say the water caught first."

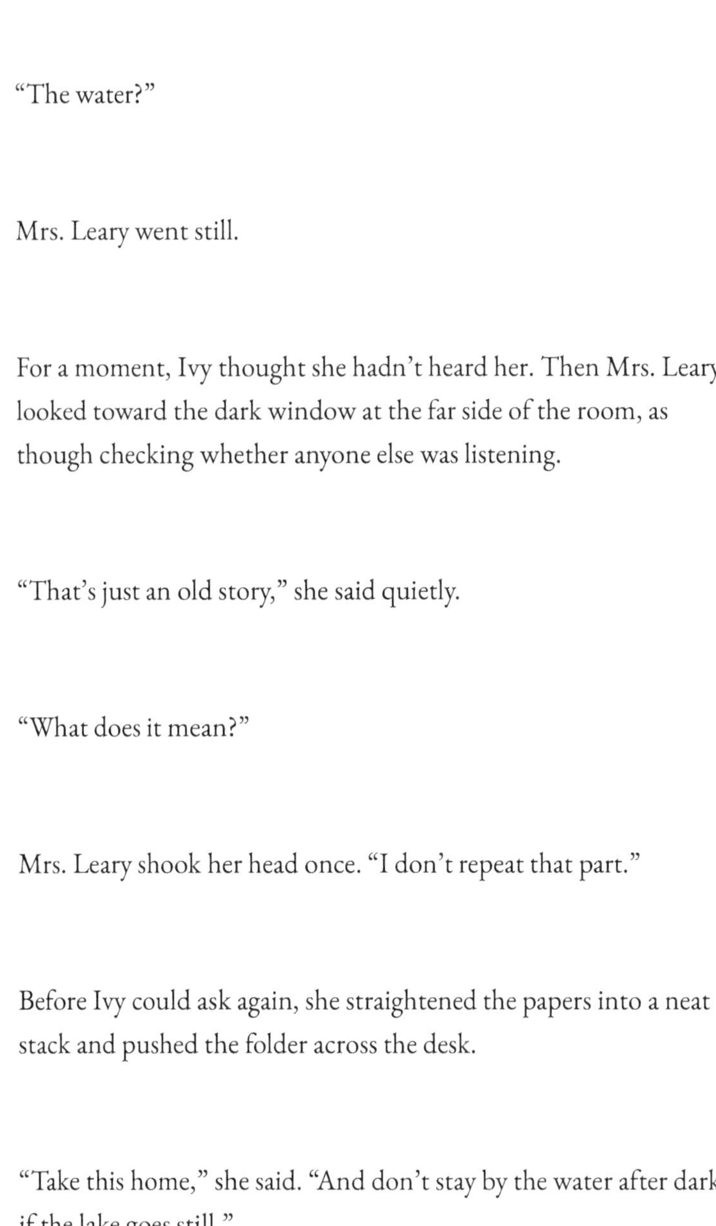

“The water?”

Mrs. Leary went still.

For a moment, Ivy thought she hadn’t heard her. Then Mrs. Leary looked toward the dark window at the far side of the room, as though checking whether anyone else was listening.

“That’s just an old story,” she said quietly.

“What does it mean?”

Mrs. Leary shook her head once. “I don’t repeat that part.”

Before Ivy could ask again, she straightened the papers into a neat stack and pushed the folder across the desk.

“Take this home,” she said. “And don’t stay by the water after dark if the lake goes still.”

By the time Ivy got home, the air had shifted again—heavier, wetter. Clouds hung low, flattening the light.

She parked, climbed the steps, and froze.

The lavender along the walkway gleamed damp, jeweled with moisture, though it hadn't rained. A thin mist hovered above the ground, hugging the edge of the lawn where it met the drop-off.

Something about the shape of it made her uneasy. The mist didn't move like fog; it pulsed, rising and falling in slow, rhythmic breaths.

She knelt near the edge, where the grass met the line of old stone. Beneath the haze, the soil looked darker—almost black.

And then she saw it.

At first, Ivy thought the tide had simply come in a little farther.

The dark line at the edge of the grass looked different somehow—wider than before, glistening faintly beneath the mist.

She leaned closer.

Water was seeping out from beneath the earth where the old line met the lawn. Not fast. Not enough to make a sound.

Just slowly.

Inch by inch, it slid over the grass in a thin, wavering trail.

Ivy stayed perfectly still, trying to tell herself it was only runoff, only groundwater, only the yard settling after rain.

But the trickle did not spread naturally.

It curved.

It changed direction.

It moved toward her.

So slowly she almost missed it, the narrow thread of water crept across the grass like something alive, bending around clumps of dirt and blades of lavender, always correcting itself, always finding its way back.

By the time Ivy realized what it was doing, it had nearly reached her foot.

The thin line stopped less than an inch from her bare big toe.

For one awful second, it looked like a finger hesitating before it touched her.

Shadow appeared in the doorway behind her.

Since moving to the lake, he had spent half his time begging to be let outside—crying at the screen door, weaving around her ankles, acting as though the porch was a great injustice being kept from him.

"You wanted out five minutes ago," Ivy said without looking back.

But Shadow didn't move.

His tail puffed wide. His ears flattened.

He stood rigid at the threshold, every hair along his back lifted, staring at the thin line of water in the grass.

When Ivy opened the screen door wider and stepped aside, inviting him out, he let out a low, unfamiliar growl.

Then he backed away from the doorway entirely.

Ivy whispered, "It remembers."

That night, she couldn't sleep. Every creak of the house felt amplified. When she finally dozed off near dawn, she dreamed of lanterns bobbing in dark water, the reflection of a man hammering boards under moonlight, and the sound of lavender rustling in a wind she couldn't feel.

When she woke, her coffee table was wet.

Just a single, perfect ring of water sat in the center of the wood, dark against the grain as though a glass had been resting there.

But she had not left a glass there.

Ivy touched it with her fingertips. It was cool—not condensation, not a spill.

There was a faint oily sheen across the surface, barely visible in the morning light.

And beneath the dampness, clinging to the edge of the ring, was a fine gray-black residue.

Not dirt.

Soot.

When she lifted her hand, the smell rose with it—faint, but unmistakable. Smoke. Oil. The sharp, bitter scent of something that had burned long ago.

Outside, the tide had drawn back farther than before.

Chapter Seven

The Quiet Beneath

By the third morning, Ivy had convinced herself she was imagining things.

Or maybe she'd simply been too still for too long — the quiet could do strange things to a mind that had only ever known motion.

She tried to return to her old routines. Coffee. Water the lavender. Feed Shadow. Don't look too long at the lake.

But even from the kitchen, she could *hear* it now — the faint lap of water against the hidden stones beneath the drop-off, an arrhythmic sound that somehow kept time with her pulse.

She took a deep breath. "You're fine," she muttered. "You just need people."

That afternoon, Ivy forced herself out of the house. She drove toward town, past the grove roads lined with old oaks, their limbs draped like sighs. The clouds had thickened, diffusing the sunlight into something almost metallic.

She parked outside the **Haven Hollow Library**, a squat brick building with wide front steps and a faded mural of the old ferry painted along one wall.

Elias was behind the counter, bent over a cart of returned books with a pencil tucked behind one ear. He looked up as she entered.

Something about him always struck her as oddly familiar.

It wasn't his face exactly. Elias was younger than the man in the photograph she'd found at the hotel, softer around the edges, his dark hair always falling slightly into his eyes. But there was something in the eyes themselves — that same pale gray-blue, that same watchful stillness. And his voice carried the same low, careful cadence that had unsettled her in the old recording from the hotel archives.

"The new lake-dweller returns," he said with a grin.

Ivy smiled despite herself. “You make me sound like a cryptid.”

“That depends,” he said. “Have you been sighted near the waterline at dusk? Haven Hollow takes these things very seriously. We’ve still got an active file on the Goat Woman of Mercer Road.”

Ivy stared at him.

He waited a beat.

“I’m kidding,” he said.

“You really need to work on your delivery.”

“Library humor is a niche market.” He leaned against the counter. “Do you happen to have anything on old ferry records? Mrs. Leary mentioned a fire.”

"Ferry records?" Elias repeated. "You're speaking my language. Though fair warning — local history is mostly eighty percent dust, fifteen percent missing paperwork, and five percent old men insisting their grandfather once punched a hurricane."

Ivy gave him the same polite, uncertain smile she always did when she suspected he was making a joke she was supposed to understand.

Ivy smiled, relieved to see a familiar face. "Do you happen to have anything on old ferry records? Mrs. Leary mentioned a fire."

Elias frowned slightly. "That would be in the historical section — back wall, bottom drawers. You'll find most of the town's paper records there. Don't expect much before 1900, though. The fire took nearly everything."

"The Great Fire?"

"The same. Funny thing about that one — it didn't start in town, not exactly."

He gestured toward the back of the library.

"Historical section's in the last row. Bottom drawers. If you find anything labeled 'Town Improvements Committee,' don't bother. It's forty years of arguments about benches."

"Benches?"

"You'd be surprised how passionately people can hate a gazebo."

"I'll keep that in mind."

"And if you run across Mrs. Daughtry's handwritten family history, ignore the part where she claims Haven Hollow was founded by escaped French nobility. Unless you enjoy a good conspiracy."

"You say that like there's a version that isn't a conspiracy."

Elias's mouth twitched. "Fair point."

Ivy paused. "What do you mean?"

He shrugged. "Old rumor says it started across the lake — somewhere near where you live now. The wind carried it across the water. But that's just talk."

She studied his face, searching for a hint of teasing. There wasn't one.

The records drawer smelled like dust and citrus polish. Most of the files were brittle and incomplete — fragments of lives folded into manila envelopes. She traced her finger along one marked *Town Expansion - 1922*. Inside were blueprints of the old pier site, penciled measurements, and faint notations in looping cursive.

At the bottom, nearly lost among the papers, was a torn scrap of parchment — older than the rest, darker, its edges soft as cloth.

Ivy unfolded it carefully.

Most of the ink had bled away with time, but one line remained faintly visible:

"... stones laid in memory of the Vale..."

Her breath caught.

The word snagged somewhere in her mind.

Vale.

She stared at it for a long moment, unable to place why it mattered.

Then, suddenly, she saw again the brittle newspaper clipping Mrs. Leary had shown her on the porch — the one with the missing family and the half-faded line about land once belonging to someone named Vale.

A strange chill moved through her.

Before she could piece it together, a low rumble shuddered through the floor. The building itself seemed to groan. Elias's voice called from the front, "It's just the freight train — tracks run right under us!"

But Ivy could've sworn the vibration hadn't come from below — it had come from somewhere *beneath the lake.*

When she looked up, Elias was watching her from the end of the aisle.

"You okay?" he asked.

The question should have felt ordinary.

Instead, something in the way he said it — quiet, almost hesitant — made that strange sense of familiarity return.

For just a second, with the dim library light catching his profile, he looked impossibly like the man from the photograph at the Gilded Hotel.

Julian Hart.

Then Elias shifted, and the resemblance vanished.

By evening, the rain had returned. A thin, unsteady drizzle that blurred the view beyond her porch. The lavender gleamed slick and dark; Shadow sat at the window, tail twitching at every flicker of lightning.

Ivy lit a single lamp and opened her notebook — the one she'd been using to track every odd thing since she moved in.

She wrote:

- The waterline is lower again.
- The mist rises at night.
- The man with the fishing pole hasn't moved.
- The sound — three beats, silence. Three beats again.

Then she hesitated, pen hovering above the paper, before adding a final line:

The water remembers. But of what?

Outside, thunder rolled across the lake — deep, distant, and wrong. Not a crack, not a boom. It was a *knock.*

Three times. vy looked toward the window.

Across the narrow canal behind the house, something moved through the rain.

For a split second, she thought the fisherman was standing on the surface of the water.

Her heart lurched.

Then lightning flashed again, and she saw it — not water, but a narrow, dark boat drifting almost soundlessly along the canal. It sat so low in the water it nearly disappeared beneath him.

The shape of it looked wrong somehow. Older. Hand-carved. Like something hollowed from a single tree trunk long before roads or bridges had ever existed here.

The fisherman stood motionless inside it, one hand resting on the pole.

Even across the canal, Ivy had the terrible feeling that he was looking directly at her.

Shadow lifted his head and hissed.

THE HAVEN HOLLOW CHRONICLE

Est. 1914 – Serving the Chain Since the Boom
November 14, 1921

GREAT BLAZE CONSUMES HAVEN HOLLOW'S FERRY

By Marianne Ellis, Staff Writer

Haven Hollow—around 8 p m. evening, the town's lone ferry a engulf in flames while bocked at the original prie, last week—while the lakeshore went rested on the water's surface.

Witnesses show stanners newk shared quickly, by time today's arrival. It was beyond saving- "One minute if was there, and the next, there was nothing but scored slaw."

Origns underthrought the origins which incinerated the ferry within minutes. Captain Barry O'Malley, 64, was the sole casuall: He had been working late—overseeing repairs to the vessel, and succumbed to death.

A life-long pilot of the Chain ferry service, ⁝to be saved, as the lefoboat way for this report. an 'there was nothing but sinoke." Simid, said Famle s tIK.

Sanctional tid-endaved Tuesday before anunknown origins osisted the ferry within minutes.

"one minute it was there, and the next, there was nothing but smoke." She said the "snapping and whooshing" sounded.

The fire, winknownd lossly wintd of minutes. Captain Barry O'Malley, 64, was the sole man overseeing repalry to his weaken and was hurrihed to the flames. Lifelong pllot of the Chain seryice—an odorous but indespensable—ferry, known as "the lifeblood of haven."

Mayor Edwin Lanpher said one statement as Captain O'Malley—never married, are in Wisconsin. "No foul play was suspected. but-due to no available backup vessels or funds for new craft.

Even when fire fades, the lake remembers.

Chapter Eight

The Echo Beneath the Floor

That night, Ivy dreamed of footsteps.

Not above her or below her, but *through* her — like sound carried through bone. Each one soft, deliberate, the faint tap of a hammer driving something deep into unseen wood.

When she woke, the air inside the house was heavy, close. The lavender outside her window glowed faintly in the fog, their outlines sharp against the gray. She sat up, half expecting to hear the three knocks again, but the world was still.

Then came a new sound — a hollow creak, low and drawn-out. At first, she thought it was the old settling of boards, but the rhythm was wrong. It was circular. Measured. Like the tide.

By late morning, the fog hadn't lifted. She wrapped herself in a sweater and wandered to the edge of the yard. The grass was slick with dew; her shoes left prints that filled almost immediately with shallow water.

The drop-off looked different today.
The stones — the ones she'd only ever seen faintly under the surface — now jutted slightly above the waterline, glistening. The lake had retreated again.

She crouched and touched one of the stones. It was smooth, but not from erosion — from *use.*

Something clinked beside her.
A small object rolled from between two stones and came to rest near her shoe: a rusted nail, thin and bent. She picked it up carefully, brushing the silt away.

Its head was hammered flat by hand. Old. Pre-industrial, maybe.

She looked back toward her house. A flicker of motion passed by the front window — a shadow, quick but definite.
"Shadow?" she called.

Her cat appeared on the porch a second later, stretching, eyes fixed not on her but on the water. His tail bristled.

Ivy followed his gaze.

The reflection of her house rippled once... then stilled.

Something was wrong.

Ivy looked up sharply at the real house.

The porch was empty. The curtains still. Nothing moved behind the windows.

Slowly, she looked back down at the water.

The reflection still wasn't right.

For just a second, she could have sworn there was a figure standing in the upstairs window — not in the house itself, only in the wavering dark of the lake.

She blinked.

The image broke apart into ripples.

That afternoon, she decided to drive into town again — not for research this time, but to breathe air that didn't feel like it was listening.

The coffee shop on Main was half full, warm with the smell of cinnamon, espresso, and rain-damp coats. The bell over the door gave a tired ring as Ivy stepped inside.

Marla was already there near the front window, one ankle crossed over the other, perfectly at ease in the way only people who had lived somewhere forever seemed to be. She wore gold hoops, a cream sweater, and the kind of confidence Ivy always admired in other women.

A steaming mug sat in front of her.

"Your usual?" Ivy asked as she slid into the seat.

"Hot comfort tea, vanilla creamer, and vanilla collagen," Marla said. "Because if I'm going to spiral, I'm going to do it with healthy skin."

Ivy laughed for the first time all day.

"Girl," Marla said, pointing lightly at her with her spoon, "you look like you've seen a ghost."

Ivy managed a laugh. "Just getting used to lake life." "That'll do it," Marla said. "And this place puts extra sugar in the coffee. That's why everybody keeps coming back."

"I heard that," called the owner from behind the counter.

Mrs. Barlow appeared in the doorway carrying a tray of muffins, her gray curls escaping from a loose clip.

"Don't you go scaring off my new customers with your nonsense," she said.

“You mean the ghost stories or the coffee?” Marla asked.

Mrs. Barlow pointed the muffin tray at her. “Both.”

The two women laughed, and for a moment the room felt ordinary again.

Marla sipped her drink. “Oh, that’ll do it. Haven Hollow’s got its moods. You’re by the south shore, right? Down by the old Vale property?”

The name pricked her spine. “Vale?”

Marla nodded. “Yeah, Edwin Vale. My great-granddaddy used to say that whole patch was built over his workshop. They say the old boards are still down there, somewhere under the water. He was the one that—”

Marla paused, studying Ivy’s face. “You look like you already know.”

“Just something I read,” Ivy said softly.

Marla leaned closer. “Well, if you believe the stories, the man worked himself to death building that dock. Some folks say his spirit never left the lake. Others say it wasn’t him that burned — it was the water, and it took him with it.”

Ivy's mouth went dry. "The water burned."

"Yeah. Weird, right? Anyway, if the house starts knocking, maybe just knock back."

Marla grinned, trying to make it a joke. But Ivy couldn't laugh.

That night, the sound returned.

Three knocks.
Silence.
Three more.

She set her mug down on the coffee table and waited. The air seemed to hum around her, every nerve tuned to that pulse.

Shadow stood at the doorway, tail flicking, eyes fixed on the floorboards beneath the rug.

Then the sound came again — not from the lake this time.

From under her feet.

Slow. Deliberate.

Knock.

Knock.

Knock.

The mug on the coffee table trembled.

Dark tea rippled across its surface in widening circles, like something had dropped a stone into the center.

Shadow backed away from the rug and sat abruptly on his hind legs, ears pitched forward, every muscle locked in attention.

Another beat passed.

The house held its breath.

Ivy whispered, barely audible, "I hear you."

And somewhere beneath the house, the water answered.

Chapter Nine

The Lake Dreams

Ivy didn't so much sleep as go still.

The house lay quiet around her, every surface holding its breath. When morning finally pressed thin light through the blinds, Shadow rose from the foot of the bed and paced the windowsill, tail switching like a metronome set just off time.

She made coffee. She made herself move—laundry in the basket, email tabs open and closed, a list written and immediately forgotten. The air had that early sweetness again, lavender lifting through the open windows, the faint mineral tang that came whenever water met heat. The scent should've calmed her. Instead it folded over her shoulders like a question.

A photo frame on the bookshelf leaned a degree to the left. She straightened it. A mug on the counter trembled the slightest bit as the fridge kicked on, then settled as if deciding not to fall. It was nothing—explainable things—but she felt every one of them, the way you feel a word on the tip of your tongue.

"Normal," she told herself. "We are doing normal."

From somewhere deep in the quiet, three slow beats answered her memory. Silence. Three again. She swallowed, set down her cup, and stepped onto the porch.

The morning was milk-pale, fog lingering in ribbons across the yard. At the edge where the boards met the drop-off, something caught the light: a small iron loop sunk flush into an older plank near the corner, the grain around it darker than the rest.

She crouched. The ring was rough under her fingers, hand-forged, the curve of it hammered flat by someone who knew the weight of rope and wet wood. At its base, the boards wore a crescent of shadow—old scorch, maybe, or oil that had seeped and settled and never quite left.

Ivy tugged once. It held.

A thin thread of scent rose—sour lamp oil, faint smoke, water left too long in a metal bucket. It arrived so suddenly she closed her eyes against it.

The porch fell away.

Lanterns bobbed above black water, their light smearing into gold across the lake.

Wet rope slapped against wood. Men shouted somewhere beyond the fog.

"Hold her—"

"Steady!"

Then she saw him.

A man stood at the far edge of the dock, his outline broken by smoke and lantern glow. One hand gripped the railing so tightly the knuckles showed pale even through the dark.

The skin along the back of that hand looked wrong — blistered and split, the cuff of his sleeve singed black.

He was trying to make his way down toward the water.

Another step.

Another.

Then the boards beneath him flashed with sudden light.

For one terrible second, the lake reflected him clearly.

Not his face.

Only the shape of him bending toward the water, one ruined hand locked around the railing as the flames rose around his legs.

The lake wore fire like silk.

She jerked back, palms flat on the boards, breath sawing the quiet.

“I saw it,” she whispered to no one. “You showed me.”

Shadow stood in the doorway behind her, pupils wide, ears pitched forward. He didn’t blink.

By late afternoon, the light had gone pewter. She needed air that didn’t feel like it was listening, so she laced her shoes and followed the loop around the canal.

The birds were gone. No sentry line, no spoon bills dragging silt—just a hush that felt heavier for their absence.

He was there, though. The man sat in his spot on the bank behind a neighboring yard, legs folded, fishing line slack on water that barely covered mud. Long dark locks brushed his shoulders. He didn't look at her until she was almost past. His boots were wet.

Not damp from morning grass. Wet enough that the leather gleamed dark around the soles.

But he was too far from the water for that.

His thumb rubbed absently at the edge of his fishing reel, metal clicking softly under the pressure. Not nervous — just occupied. Like he needed something solid beneath his hands.

"You saw it," he said.

Ivy stopped. "What?"

He tipped his chin toward the lake, not unkind. "It's waking up."

He smiled then, just slightly.

For half a second, something about it looked wrong.

Not cruel. Not angry.

Just unfamiliar — as though the expression belonged to someone else wearing his face.

Then it was gone.

"It...?" She shook her head. "You mean it remembers him."

The man didn't answer. He watched the surface like he expected it to speak.

They stood there with the quiet between them until a truck rattled somewhere beyond the grove road. Ivy found her voice. "Why are you fishing when there's no water?"

He smiled, the ghost of one. "There's always water. Sometimes it just steps back to listen." He reeled in nothing and set the hook again. "You should go before dark." Ivy frowned. "Why?"

The fisherman looked past her toward the house.

"Because once the lights start in the upstairs window," he said quietly, "she never sleeps."

Ivy felt the blood leave her face.

She had never told anyone about the shape she'd thought she'd seen in the reflection.

Before she could ask what he meant, he cast the line again.

When she turned for home, she glanced back once and faltered. The waterline along the mud had crept up an inch, maybe two, slick and new where it hadn't been a minute before.

Back on the porch, the world felt thinner, as if a page had been turned while she wasn't looking. She set her keys down and knelt by the corner plank.

A ring of moisture circled the iron loop—a perfect tide mark no wider than a coin. It gleamed in the dim like a breath on glass, brightening and fading with the same patient rhythm she'd felt under her floor.

Ivy leaned close, the lavender and the faint tang of oil braided in the air. She didn't mean to speak, but the words left her anyway, soft enough to be mistaken for thought.

"What do you want me to remember?"

The ring brightened once, then stilled.

For the first time, Ivy realized she wasn't uncovering history.

History was uncovering her.

Somewhere far across the lake, almost too faint to hear, a bell rang.

Not a church bell.

A hard, urgent clang. Old-fashioned. Metallic.

The kind of sound a fire engine might have made long before sirens existed.

The scent of smoke drifted through the lavender.

When Ivy looked toward the road, there was nothing there.

Chapter Ten

When the Lake Spoke

That night, Ivy didn't bother turning on the lamp.
She sat on the couch in the dark, watching the faint glimmer of moonlight play across the windowpane. Shadow had curled into a crescent on the armrest, but his tail flicked, restless. Every now and then, he'd open his eyes, pupils wide as ink, and stare toward the back door.

Outside, the air was heavy again — too still for Florida, the kind of stillness that precedes rain or revelation.

It started as a vibration under her feet. Not a sound — a feeling. A low hum, as though something massive had awakened deep below. Then, faintly, the rhythm returned.

Knock.
Knock.
Knock.

The same slow, patient cadence.

But this time, it wasn't under the floor. It was all around her.

Ivy rose, heart steady but fast. She stepped onto the porch barefoot. The boards were damp, and the night smelled of lavender and rain that hadn't fallen.

The lake was alive with light.

Not bright — not unnatural — but faint, flickering, as though lanterns drifted just beneath the surface. The pattern moved like a current, weaving in deliberate lines that shimmered, vanished, then reappeared in new shapes.

She walked to the edge, stopping where the yard ended and the drop-off began.

For a moment, she thought she saw people — silhouettes under the surface, blurred by water and light.

Then the image sharpened.

The lake no longer reflected the present.

It showed her the pier as it had been.

Lanterns burned along a wide wooden dock, their light flickering gold across wet planks darkened by years of use. Thick rope was coiled along the edges, iron rings bolted deep into the boards, slick with water and time. The structure stretched farther than anything that stood there now — long, deliberate, built to carry weight.

People moved across it in hurried lines.

At first, it felt like a festival — the faint echo of music, the glow of lanterns, the sweet, airy smell of spun sugar drifting through the air. Something like cotton candy. Something like caramel just beginning to burn.

Then the scene twisted.

The sweetness turned sharp.

Smoke bled into the air.

The smell of burnt sugar thickened into something darker — scorched wood, hot oil, meat left too long over flame.

The lanterns didn't flicker anymore. They flared.

People began to run.

Footsteps pounded across the boards in uneven bursts, some fast, some stumbling, the sound carrying through the water like distant thunder. Voices rose — not words at first, just urgency. Then shouts. Then something closer to panic.

A woman slipped near the edge. Someone reached for her.

A man shouted for a rope.

Another voice called from the far end — steady, trying to hold order against the chaos.

The boards beneath them glowed faintly at the seams.

Then brighter.

The water caught the light and held it, reflecting fire back onto the structure until it looked as though the lake itself had begun to burn.

The original pier.

The one that had burned.

The lantern-light pulsed once, twice, three times.

A voice — not loud, but near enough to vibrate the air between her and the water — whispered:

"Do you hear it now?"

Ivy froze. "Who are you?"

The question startled her. She hadn't meant to speak.

For a heartbeat, she wanted to turn back inside, lock the door, and call someone — the power company, Elias, anyone who could reduce light to wiring and vibration to weather.

She could still choose that version of the night.

Instead, she stayed where she was.

No answer. Just a ripple across the reflection, the light bending in on itself like a breath drawn and held.

Shadow meowed sharply behind her — low, warning, guttural. She turned. The house was dark. Every bulb inside had gone out.

When she looked back, the light on the water had formed words — or something close to words. Not letters, not quite — more like impressions, half-familiar shapes that tugged at memory. She felt them instead of reading them.

It wasn't the fire. It was the remembering.

The words didn't feel heard. They felt placed.

Ivy's breath broke.

Her hands trembled where they hung at her sides, fingers curling and uncurling like she didn't know what to do with them.

The images didn't leave her right away. They clung — the sound of feet striking wood, the smell of smoke, the way the light had turned from warm to violent in a matter of seconds.

Someone had died there.

More than someone.

And the lake had kept all of it.

Ivy swallowed hard, her throat tight, her chest aching with a grief that didn't belong to her and yet somehow did.

She felt it then — not just the memory, but the weight of it. The quiet accumulation of everything that had happened before she arrived, everything that had shaped the place she now called home.

Her vision blurred.

She didn't realize she was crying until a tear slipped free and hit the porch at her feet.

The lavender along the walkway stirred though no wind blew. The scent thickened until it was nearly tangible, sweet and sharp.

Then, as quickly as it had appeared, the light winked out. The lake fell still.

Ivy stood alone in the dark, the hum gone, the silence heavier than sound.

She whispered, "I hear you."

And in the quiet, the faintest ripple touched the shore — like the exhale of something that had been holding its breath for more than a century.

Chapter Eleven

The Keeper's Story

The morning after the lights on the lake, everything felt unnaturally clean — as if the air had been rinsed. The water gleamed smooth as glass. Even the lavender looked new, every petal rinsed pale, dew clinging to its tips like punctuation.

Ivy stood at the porch rail, notebook in hand, and watched the sunlight shift across the water. The fear from the night before had cooled into something steadier, almost reverent.

She started writing. Not for proof this time. Just so she wouldn't forget.

The lake spoke.
The light was not fire.
He built something, and it remembered.

Shadow brushed her leg, his fur warm against the morning breeze. Somewhere far off, a hammer struck — faint, rhythmic, the sound of construction. Or memory repeating itself.

By noon, she found herself in the Historical Society again.

Mrs. Leary looked up, brows raised. "You're becoming a regular, dear."

"I need to see everything you have on Edwin Vale," Ivy said. "Not the fire. The man."

Mrs. Leary hesitated, then led her toward a side room lined with filing drawers older than the building itself. "There's one box that never got indexed. Settlement-era personal effects. Could be junk. Could be treasure."

The box was marked in fading ink: *1890–1894 (Personal).*

Inside lay the detritus of someone's life — brittle envelopes, smudged ledgers, paper held together by rusted pins. Ivy sifted through until something caught her eye: a sheet of parchment torn from a notebook, the ink thin but legible.

> *"The stones must remember, or else the water will forget."*

Below the line, a name signed in bold, confident loops: **E. Vale.**

Her pulse stuttered. She reached deeper into the box and found a pressed sprig of lavender, brown and delicate, tucked between the pages of an old inventory ledger.

Mrs. Leary peered over her shoulder. “Funny place to keep a flower.”

Ivy smiled faintly. “Maybe not.”

Together they unfolded the ledger, scanning the entries. Vale’s handwriting was neat, formal — lists of stone shipments, lamp oil orders, repair notes. The kind of writing that belonged to someone who believed structure could hold the world in place.

But the ink changed near the bottom of one page. The lines lost their precision, slanting slightly, as though written in a moment that didn’t allow for care.

“For Marianne — may the lake take only what it’s given.”

Ivy traced the edge of the page with her finger.

There was a smudge near the margin, faint but deliberate — the impression of a thumb pressed into still-wet ink. Larger than she expected. A builder's hand. Someone used to lifting, bracing, holding weight.

Tucked into the fold beside it, the pressed lavender shifted slightly.

She imagined it fresh once — cut and handed over absentmindedly, or kept carefully between pages by someone who wanted to remember a moment that wouldn't last.

Marianne.

Not just a name.

Someone he had built for.

"His wife?" Mrs. Leary asked softly.

"Has to be," Ivy murmured. "He wasn't warning us," Ivy said quietly. "He was trying to leave her something that would last."

Mrs. Leary's eyes warmed. "Maybe that's what this place is — promises that never quite stop echoing."

By the time Ivy returned home, clouds had thickened, though the air stayed dry. The world felt suspended, like the sky was waiting for her to move first.

She placed the pressed lavender on the porch rail and set a candle beside it. The match hissed, and the small flame leaned immediately toward the lake.

For a moment, the scent of oil returned — faint, spectral — then vanished, replaced by something clean and metallic, like fresh rain on stone.

She whispered, "You can rest now."

The words felt heavier than she expected.

Saying them meant something had changed — not just in the water, but in her.

She would have to decide what to do with what she knew. Whether to tell the town. Whether to leave it undisturbed.

Not every memory wanted an audience.

The candle flickered once, then steadied.

From somewhere across the water, a faint echo answered — not a knock, not a voice, but a resonance. A low hum that carried more peace than sound.

Shadow emerged from under the chair, circling once before settling at her feet. The lavender swayed, releasing its quiet perfume into the evening.

Ivy exhaled slowly, feeling the house around her — the floor's gentle pulse, the boards creaking in time with her own breath. The fear was gone. The mystery remained.

As dusk fell, the wind shifted. The lake sighed against the stones, and from far across the water came the softest chime — one note, distant and deliberate, followed by another.

Bells.

Not from the pier. Not from town.
From the water itself.

Ivy closed her eyes and listened until she couldn't tell where the sound ended and her heartbeat began.

Chapter Twelve

The Hollow Bells

Dawn came like a held breath released.

Light spilled over the lake in long, pale bands, softening the hard edge of the drop-off until water and land looked sewn together with thread you couldn't see. The lavender opened to it, each blossom catching dew like a syllable.

Ivy stood at the porch rail and listened. No knocking. No hammering. Only the smallest hush—the sound a page makes when it's turned.

She brewed coffee and let it cool in her hands, drifting from window to door and back again as the house settled around her. The air felt rinsed. The faint metallic tang that had haunted the last few weeks was gone, replaced by clean morning and the green of wet grass. Shadow moved like a shadow should—silent, curious—pausing at the threshold to test the day.

Across the water, the Haven Pier slept under its own reflection. Nothing strange, nothing strained. Just light, and the sense that something vast had finished speaking.

Then, from somewhere far across the Links, a single note rang—low, clear, and impossible.
A bell.

It wasn't loud, but it traveled the way truth does—straight through. Another followed, softer, like an answer. Ivy stepped onto the grass and felt the sound in her ribs. It faded, then returned, as if the lake were breathing with her.

She followed the notes down the yard, past the lavender, to the line where the stones waited under a shallow skin of water. The lake was modestly higher than yesterday, just enough to lace light through the first inch of shore. Something pale winked between two stones and caught.

A small glass bottle.

It wasn't elaborate—no sailor's knot, no dramatic stopper—just river-glass thick with age, a corroded cap, and inside, the ghost of a page. Ivy knelt. Water cooled her knees through the denim. She worked the cap until it gave with a tired sigh and tapped the bottle against her palm until the paper slid into her hand like a breath.

The ink had broken into islands, but three words held fast, elegant and steady, as if written for weather:

For those who listen.

She smiled without meaning to. “I hear you.”

Behind her, Shadow settled on the porch, tail curled around himself like punctuation. A breeze pressed through the lavender and carried their scent down to the water; the blossoms nodded like a congregation.

Ivy set the bottle on the rail to dry and opened her notebook on the step. She wrote what she wanted to keep: the bells, the clean morning, the way the lake felt finished and awake at the same time. She added Vale’s name, and Marianne’s, and a line she didn’t plan to show anyone:

Water remembers. So do we.

Later, needing to move, Ivy slipped on her shoes and followed the loop around the canal.

The neighborhood felt lighter than it had the day before. Easier.

She didn’t realize where she was headed until she saw the house.

The fisherman’s house.

She slowed.

The back of it faced the canal, just as it always had. But now, in the full light of day, something felt... off.

The glass patio doors stood bare. No curtains. No furniture. Nothing inside at all.

Ivy stepped closer to the fence line, peering through the glass.

Empty.

Not newly moved out. Not recently cleaned.

Just... empty.

She continued around the curve of the path, coming to the front of the house.

No car in the drive. No sign of movement. No dogs.

The yard had the same untouched look as the inside — like no one had ever quite settled into it.

“Strange, isn’t it?”

Ivy turned.

Marla approached from the opposite direction, her pace easy, hands tucked into the pockets of her sweater.

“I was just—” Ivy hesitated. “I thought someone lived here.”

Marla followed her gaze to the house.

“That one?” she said. “No. That place has been empty for a while now.”

Ivy felt something cold settle under her ribs. “Empty?”

“Yeah,” Marla said. “One of the last ones built on this stretch. Never really stuck with anyone. People come, people go. Or they just... don’t stay long.”

Ivy shook her head slightly. “I’ve seen someone here. A man. He fishes along the canal.”

Marla frowned.

“I’ve never seen anyone fishing there,” she said.

Ivy opened her mouth, then stopped. In her mind she could see him as clearly as the canal itself: the faded green shirt, the long dark hair stirring in the breeze, the two dogs waiting in the grass. The careful, unhurried way he baited the hook.

“I know what I saw,” she said quietly.

Marla looked back toward the canal, her expression unreadable.

"Not on that side," she said after a moment.

A breeze moved through the grass between them.

Ivy followed Marla's gaze toward the water. The canal lay flat and bright in the morning sun, empty except for the shimmer of light at its edge.

She let it go. The ordinary belonged here, too.

By late morning, the sun lay warm on the porch boards. She made a place for the bottle on the windowsill beside her notes. The glass threw a small oval of light onto the wall, a quiet halo that moved as the day did.

When the breeze rose again, it carried no ash, no oil. Only lavender. Only lake.

Afternoon came easy. She folded linens for the guest room, measured curtain rods she might never order, and paused when the light shifted the way it does just before evening. The world felt unburdened—not emptied, exactly, but set down.

As dusk slid across the water, the bells tolled once more—two notes this time, close together, then nothing. Not a farewell. A benediction.

Ivy stood at the threshold—half shelter, half horizon—and let the quiet take its shape around her.

For the first time in her life, she didn't feel like she was starting over.
She felt like she'd finally come home.

Not because the lake had quieted.

Not because the bells had stopped.

But because she no longer needed them to explain themselves.

Some places don't ask to be solved.

They ask to be kept.

As Ivy turned to go back inside, something caught her eye.

The iron ring at the edge of the porch — the one set into the old plank — was damp.

Not from rain.

Not from dew.

Just a thin, perfect circle of moisture, darkening the wood around it.

Ivy stood there for a moment, watching it.

Then, faintly, from somewhere across the canal — not the lake — came the softest sound.

Water shifting.

As if something had just stepped out of it.

Water doesn’t forget. It simply waits for someone who listens.

Also by Lula Starling

The Gilded Hotel

Book One of the Haven Hollow Mystery series.

Amazon | Barnes & Noble

Front and Center: Unlocking Your Main Character Energy

An affirmation word-search experience guiding you from *Starling to Supernova.*

Amazon | Barnes & Noble

Hard Sudoku Book for Adults

100 puzzles to sharpen your focus and quiet your mind.

Amazon

Explore more books, updates, and exclusive releases

Scan below to visit the official Lula Starling website

Acknowledgments

To the quiet places that hold stories long after the world stops listening.

To the city of Winter Haven, whose lakes whispered the first line of this story and never stopped.

To the readers who walk with Ivy—thank you for hearing what the water had to say.

And to every dreamer rebuilding themselves piece by piece: may you find peace in the echoes that call you home.

— *Lula Starling*

About the Author

Lula Starling writes for those standing between who they were and who they're becoming. Her work explores transformation through reflection—whether in poetry, puzzles, or prose—and invites readers to pause long enough to see how far they've already come.

When she isn't writing, Lula enjoys exploring nature, visiting neighboring towns, and attending community events that celebrate the slow, intentional pace of life she came to Central Florida to embrace. These moments of stillness and discovery often inspire the settings and emotions that bloom throughout her stories.

Follow Lula Starling's creative journey:
Facebook – The Lula Starling Experience
🎥 YouTube – The Lula Starling Experience
🎬 Instagram – @TheLulaStarlingExperience

Where Creativity Roots and Stories Bloom.

Intentionally Left Blank

www.ingramcontent.com/pod-product-compliance
Lightning Source LLC
LaVergne TN
LVHW010904110826
845149LV00005B/1467

* 9 7 9 8 9 9 4 3 5 5 7 5 6 *